Thomas, James and the Dirty Work

Based on *The Railway Series* **by The Rev. W. Awdry**

EGMONT

We bring stories to life

First published in Great Britain 2009 by Egmont UK Limited
239 Kensington High Street, London W8 6SA

Thomas the Tank Engine & Friends™

CREATED BY BRITT ALLCROFT

Based on The Railway Series by The Reverend W Awdry
© 2009 Gullane (Thomas) LLC. A HIT Entertainment company.

Thomas the Tank Engine & Friends and Thomas & Friends are trademarks of Gullane (Thomas) Limited.
Thomas the Tank Engine & Friends and Design is Reg. U.S. Pat. & Tm. Off.

NORTH EAST LINCOLNSHIRE LIBRARIES

CLE		
GCL	NUN	
GCR	SCO	
GRA	SLS	
HUM		
IM		
L		

12|10

D0244101

All rights reserved.
ISBN 978 1 4052 4428 2
1 3 5 7 9 10 8 6 4 2
Printed in China

James the Red Engine is proud of his shiny red paintwork and gleaming brass dome.

He always likes to look his best.

And he likes his friends to know he's the smartest engine on Sodor!

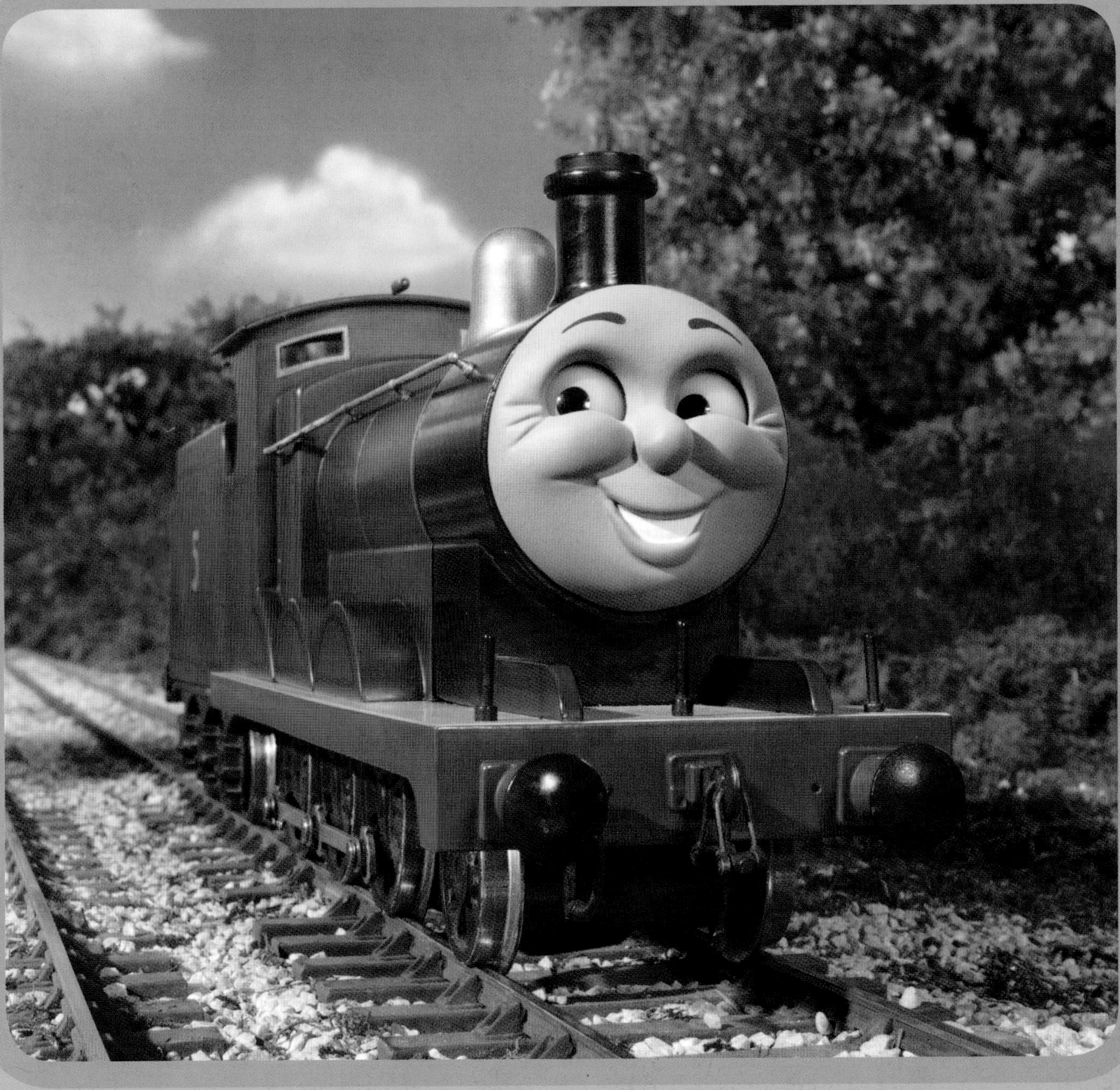

One morning, James puffed in to Tidmouth Sheds. He'd been to the Fitter's Yard for repairs and was excited to get back to work.

"I hope I get an important job today," James wheeshed to Thomas, Percy and Emily.

Just then, The Fat Controller arrived. "I need an engine for a Special," he boomed. "The Mayor must be taken to the Festival of Lights at the Scottish Castle."

"I'm the perfect engine for that job, Sir," James boasted.

"Very well, James," said The Fat Controller. "You can take the Mayor."

James was delighted!

The Fat Controller told Thomas, Emily and Percy they could go to the Festival when they had finished their jobs.

"I can't wait to go to the Festival," peeped Percy.
"Neither can I," wheeshed Emily.
"You'll look splendid, James!" puffed Thomas.

James was looking forward to making his grand entrance.

"We have lots of jobs to do first," peeped Percy.

"You haven't anything to do all day, James," puffed Emily. "Will you help us, please?"

"Me?" snorted James. "I need to look really smart when I arrive with my important passenger."
And he puffed proudly away to the washdown.

At the washdown, James was very happy. He enjoyed having his boiler brushed and his cab cleaned.

Percy stopped to talk to James on his way to the Quarry.

"I still have lots of work to do," he puffed. "Will you help me, James?"

"Sorry, Percy," sniffed James. "It's much more important that I look smart. Next, I need to be polished."

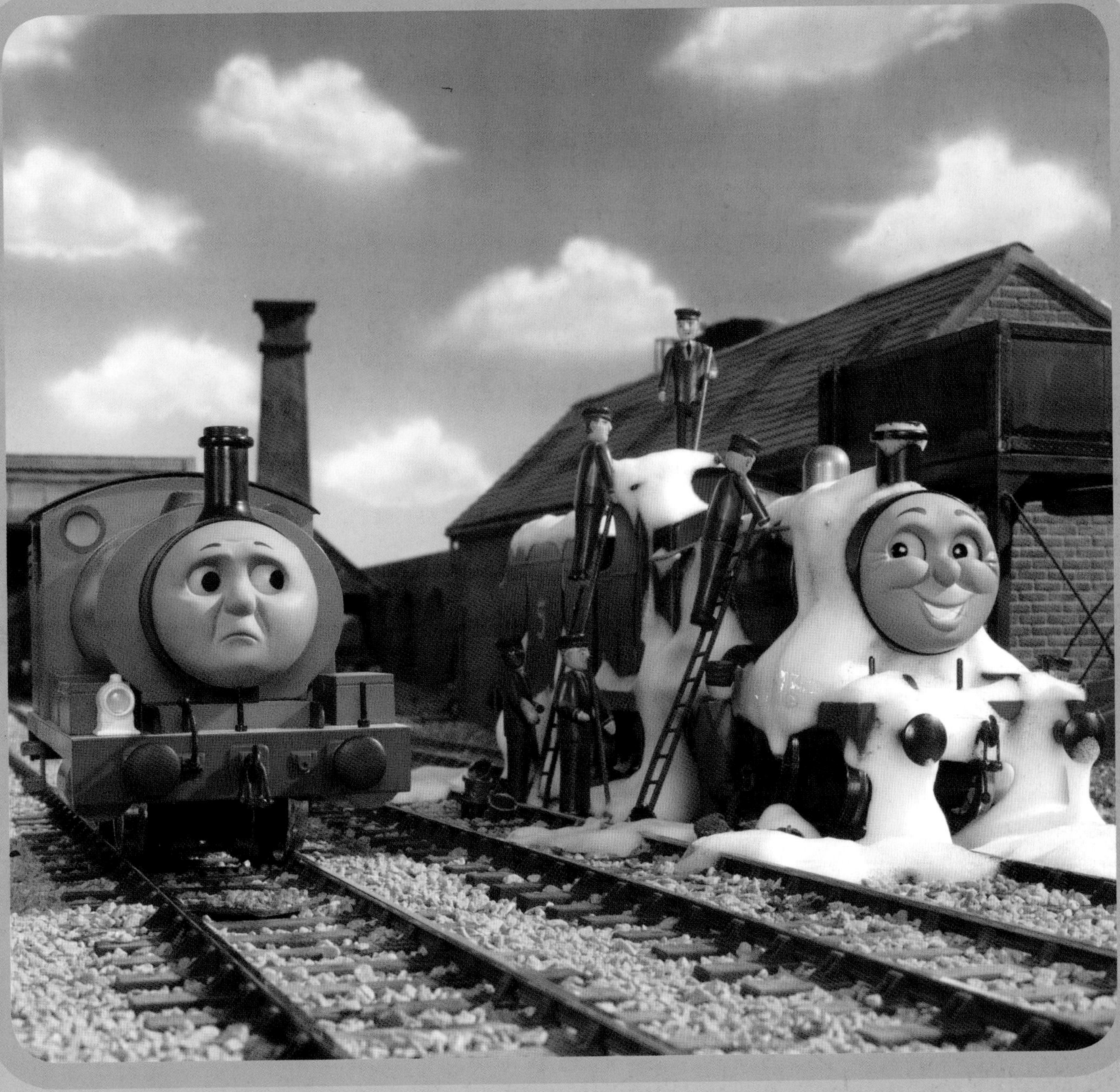

Soon, James was being polished until he shone.

"Don't forget to buff up my buffers," he said, bossily.

Just then, Thomas puffed up with a long line of coal trucks. Cling-clang, cling-clang went the trucks.

"Those trucks look troublesome!" laughed James.

"They are," huffed Thomas. "Will you help me, James?"

"Sorry, Thomas," said James. "I need to look smart for my important passenger. Now I have to get my funnel swept."

As his crew set to work sweeping James' funnel, James smelt something fishy.

"Bust my buffers!" he cried. "Whatever's that?"

It was Emily. She was pulling trucks full of crates of fish very slowly.

"These are very heavy. Will you help me, James?" she puffed, wearily.

"Certainly not," sniffed James. "I need to have some special flags fitted. They will make me look smart when I arrive at the Festival."

Before long, James was ready.

His flags fluttered ... his buffers beamed ... and he shone from funnel to footplate.

Everyone he passed cheered and waved.

"I am the smartest engine ever!" James puffed, proudly.

On the way to collect the Mayor, James passed the Scottish Castle.

It looked wonderful. Everything was ready for the Festival, and The Fat Controller was waiting on the platform.

But there were no engines! James was surprised.

"Where are Thomas and Percy and Emily?" James cried.

"They haven't finished their work," boomed The Fat Controller, loudly. "So they won't be able to come to the Festival."

James felt terrible. "I must help my friends. Otherwise they won't see how splendid I look," he said.

James found Thomas. He was still having trouble with his coal trucks.

"I'm going to miss the Festival," Thomas sighed.

"No, you're not," James replied, "because I'm going to help you!"

And that's just what he did.

James buffered up to the trucks and helped Thomas finish his work . . . even though his shiny red paintwork got covered in coal dust!

Next, James found Percy in the Quarry. Percy was struggling to pull some heavy trucks of clay.

"I'm going to miss the Festival," Percy sighed, sadly.

"No, you're not," puffed James, "because I'm going to help you!"

And that's just what James did . . . even though he got covered in quarry dust!

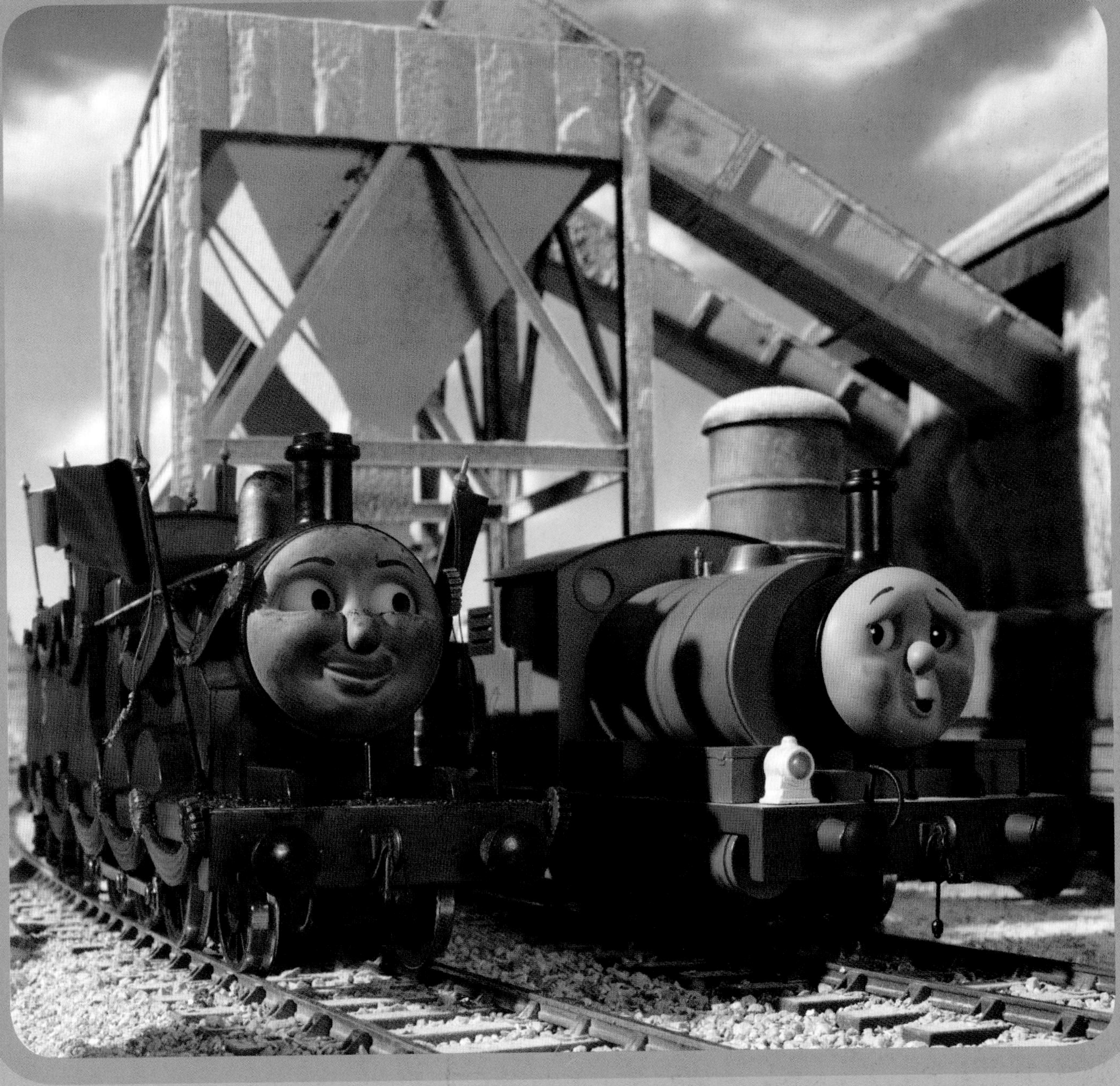

Then, James found Emily at the Junction.

"I can't pull the fish trucks any further, James. They are too heavy! I'm going to miss the Festival," she peeped, sadly.

"No, you're not!" puffed James, "because I'm going to help you!"

And that's just what James did . . . even though he knew he would end up smelling of fish!

With the day's work done, it was time for the Festival.

At the Scottish Castle, the brass band was gathered . . .

a red carpet was ready . . . and so were Thomas, Percy and Emily.

They were all waiting for James to arrive with his important passenger.

"Here comes James now!" smiled Thomas.

And Percy whistled, "Pip-peep, pip!"

Everyone cheered as James arrived with the Mayor.

But James wasn't smiling. He was worried.

After helping his friends, he was dirty and smelly. He didn't feel splendid at all.

"James," said The Fat Controller. "You are . . . a very hard-working and Really Useful Engine!"

James was amazed.

"You're not cross with me, Sir?
Even though my flags are drooping
and I'm covered in coal dust and smell
of fish?" he cried.

"What matters, James," said The Fat Controller,
"is that you helped your friends and safely delivered
your important passenger. Well done!"

James was very happy.

And his friends all thought that James was still the
most splendid engine on Sodor!

Did you enjoy the story?
Can you answer these questions?

1 What colour is James' paintwork?

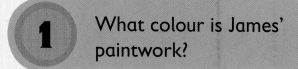

2 Who was James' important passenger?

3 What was in Thomas' trucks?

4 Which engine was pulling trucks of fish?

Answers: 1) red; 2) the Mayor; 3) coal; 4) Emily.